' ''I've got an idea,'' said the [Little Dragon]. ''You'll have to help.''

''What's the idea?'' Janet asked suspiciously.

''You get the other characters in the story out of the book and let's see if we can all agree on a different story.''

''Mmm,'' said Janet, thinking hard. ''Would you go back into the book on a permanent basis if we could find a way to change the story?''

''Oh, I would,'' the Little Dragon assured her. ''I don't like being out here with you, but it's better than being killed by that rotten old Sir George or whatever his name is.''

''All right,'' Janet said, ''I will try to help. Mind you, I didn't exactly *get* you out of the story, you just came. Maybe the others won't come.''

''We can but try,'' said the Little Dragon. ''No one can do more than their best.'' '

Janet finds herself with an unusual companion when the Little Dragon steps out of her library book and asks for help. If the Little Dragon is to be saved from Sir George's sword, Janet must help to work out a new ending to the story . . .

The Little Dragon Steps Out

ANN JUNGMAN

Illustrated by Maggie Kneen

YOUNG CORGI BOOKS

THE LITTLE DRAGON STEPS OUT

A YOUNG CORGI BOOK 0 552 525219

Originally published in Great Britain by
Young Corgi Books

PRINTING HISTORY
Young Corgi edition published 1989

This book is set in 18/24 pt Garamond
by Colset Private Limited, Singapore.

Young Corgi Books are published by Transworld Publishers Ltd., 61–63
Uxbridge Road, Ealing, London W5 5SA, in Australia by Transworld
Publishers (Australia) Pty. Ltd., 15–23 Helles Avenue, Moorebank,
NSW 2170, and in New Zealand by Transworld Publishers (N.Z.) Ltd.,
Cnr. Moselle and Waipareira Avenues, Henderson, Auckland.

Made and printed in Great Britain by
The Guernsey Press Co. Ltd., Guernsey, Channel Islands.

To Kath and family

Chapter 1

Janet sat at her desk, flicking through her school library book. It was all about a Knight and a Dragon and a Princess. 'Boring,' Janet thought to herself, and she stared out of the window.

'Janet,' said her teacher, 'what is going on outside that is so much more interesting than your book?'

'Nothing, Miss,' replied Janet weakly. She picked up her book again and, sighing, looked at it. To her amazement she noticed that where the Dragon had been in the picture was a little blank space and there, on her desk, sat a tiny creature. The Dragon had just walked out of the book and was sitting on her desk looking at her. Janet stared at the Dragon, and the Dragon stared at Janet.

'Go back,' she whispered fiercely. 'Go back into the book this minute.'

'Won't,' said the Dragon, 'jolly well won't. If you knew

what was going to happen to me in that story you wouldn't ask such a thing.'

'Why, what would happen?' asked Janet, intrigued in spite of herself.

'Don't ask,' the Little Dragon replied, covering his eyes. 'I don't even want to think about it.'

Samantha Brown, who sat near Janet, put her hand up. 'Please, Miss, Janet Evans is talking to herself.'

'I'm not,' said Janet crossly.

Samantha Brown wasn't her
favourite person.

'Yes, you were,' Samantha
insisted. 'I heard you.'

'I was not talking to myself,' Janet snapped. 'I was talking to . . .' She stopped in mid-sentence. What would happen to the Little Dragon if she told the class about him? Quickly she put the Dragon into the pocket of her dress.

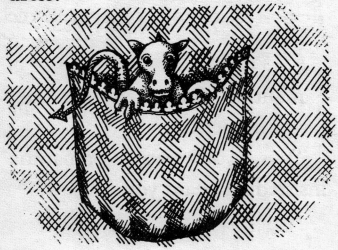

'Well, Janet,' demanded her teacher. 'Who were you talking to?'

'Myself, I suppose,' Janet muttered. 'Sorry, my mind must have wandered.' Samantha Brown giggled.

'I think you'd better go to the sick-room and lie down,' said the teacher.

'Can I take my book, please?' asked Janet desperately. She didn't want to be stuck with the

Dragon and no story to send him back to.

'Well, all right,' said her teacher, 'but you didn't seem very interested in it ten minutes ago.'

'Thank you, Miss,' mumbled Janet, and she ran out of the room, trying not to catch Samantha Brown's happy grin of triumph.

Chapter 2

Janet went into the sick-room and sat on the bed. Mrs Bird, who looked after the children when they were ill, took her temperature and found nothing wrong.

'Still, love,' said Mrs Bird, 'you'd better stay here till home time. If you're feeling off colour you won't want to play rounders.'

She went out, shutting the door and leaving Janet alone with the Little Dragon. Janet put her hand into her pocket, took the Dragon out and put him on her bed.

'I didn't like it in your pocket,' he informed her fussily. 'I didn't like it one bit. You're jolly lucky I didn't burn you.' He blew a puff of smoke at her.

'You've got a nerve to complain,' Janet replied. 'Look at all the trouble you've got me into.'

'Trouble?' moaned the Little Dragon. 'You call this trouble? You don't know what trouble is.

At least you haven't got some horrible Knight chasing you, wanting to kill you. No! You don't know what trouble is!'

'Well, what happens in the book isn't my fault!' Janet told him. 'There's nothing I can do about it. You're to go straight back into the story and no more arguing.'

'Won't,' said the Little Dragon defiantly. 'Jolly well won't. There is no way you are going to talk me into going back into that book and that is that.'

'But what am I going to do with you if you refuse to go back into the story? I'll get into trouble if there's something wrong with the book.'

'That is your problem,' the Little Dragon announced. 'The horrible Knight who wants to kill me is *my* problem, and *I* am *your* problem.'

'It's not fair,' complained Janet. 'I never asked you to come out of the book, and I *like* rounders.'

'Tough,' said the Little Dragon.

'If you're going to be horrid,' said Janet, 'I shall ignore you and read my story.'

'You can't,' the little Dragon pointed out.

'Why not?' asked Janet.

'Because, silly,' the Little Dragon continued, 'without me there *is* no story. Until I go back into the book it can't go on, and

I'm certainly not going back.'

'Oh dear,' said Janet feeling panicky. 'I don't know what to do.'

'I've got an idea,' said the Dragon. 'But you'd have to help.'

'What's the idea?' Janet asked suspiciously.

'You get the other characters out of the book and let's see if we can all agree on a different story.'

'Mmm,' said Janet, thinking hard. 'Would you go back into

the book on a permanent basis if we could find a way to change the story?'

'Oh, I would,' the Little Dragon assured her. 'I don't like being out here with you, but it's better than being killed by that rotten old Sir George or whatever his name is.'

'All right,' said Janet, 'I will try to help. Mind you, I didn't exactly *get* you out of the story, you just came. Maybe the others won't come.'

'We can but try,' said the Little Dragon. 'No one can do more than their best.'

Chapter 3

When the bell went for the end of school, Mrs Bird told Janet she should go home if she felt well enough. Janet said that she did and, clutching her book and after checking that the Little Dragon

was safely in her pocket, she set
off for home. At the school gates
Samantha Brown was waiting.

'Janet Evans is batty,' Samantha announced. 'Janet Evans talks to herself.'

'Ignore her,' hissed the Little Dragon from Janet's pocket. 'We'll deal with her later.'

Janet walked past Samantha and her friends with her nose in the air and went off home. As she walked in the door, her mother called out, 'Hello, love. Had a good day?'

'Not bad,' said Janet, wondering whether or not to tell her

mother about the Little Dragon.

'Did you win the rounders match?' asked her mother.

'I didn't play,' Janet told her. 'I was sent to the sick-room.'

'Why?' asked her mother in a concerned tone. 'What was wrong?'

'Nothing, really,' said Janet. 'I was just reading a book about a Dragon when . . .' Suddenly she felt a burning sensation on her knee.

'Ouch!' she shrieked.

'Be quiet!' hissed the Little Dragon. 'You don't have to tell her everything.'

'What's going on?' asked Janet's mother.

'I keep getting a funny burning sensation,' Janet said. ' I want to go to bed.'

'Oh dear,' said her mother. 'That's not like you. You must feel bad. Up you go. I'll bring you some tea on a tray and a nice hot-water bottle.'

Janet went upstairs and got into bed.

'That was a good idea of yours,' said the Little Dragon approvingly. 'Now we can have a whole evening to ourselves to sort out the story. You lie in bed and I'll sit on your bedside table, and we can get to work.'

'What if Mum comes up?' asked Janet.

'I'll run and hide behind your lamp,' said the Little Dragon.

'Now, as soon as she's brought up the food and things, tell her you want to be left alone and we can get on with the matter in hand.'

'Oh, all right,' Janet said, sighing heavily. 'I suppose I'll have to do what you want, but I'm fed up. I've missed rounders and now I've had to go to bed early when I am perfectly well.'

'Never mind about all that,' said the Little Dragon. 'That's all chicken feed. We've got serious

work to do to find a way to save my life.'

Janet did as the Little Dragon told her and soon they were sharing fishfingers and baked beans.

'Mmmm,' said the Little Dragon, licking his paws. 'Delicious. Now, let's try and think of a way of getting the others out of the book, so that we can plan something.'

'I don't know how to get them out,' protested Janet.

'Neither do I,' said the Little Dragon, 'but maybe if I challenge Sir George he'll rise to the bait.'

'What do you mean?' Janet asked.

'Look, you hold the book up there so that Sir George has to look at me. That's it. Right – here we go.' The Little Dragon cleared his throat.

'Sir George, it is I, the Dragon, who art speaking to thee. I challenge thee to come out from yon book, if thou darest. If thou darest not, then thou art a craven coward and a knave.'

'Now steady on, old chap,' came a voice from the book, and out stepped the Knight.

Chapter 4

Janet looked with amazement at the two tiny figures staring at each other on her duvet.

'I did it!' squeaked the Little Dragon. 'You came out.'

'I most certainly did, old chap,'

said Sir George. 'You challenged
me. Chap's got to come when
challenged.'

'Quite so,' said the Little
Dragon. 'But let me make one
thing clear to you from the word
go. I don't want to fight you.'

'You don't?' Sir George said,
looking puzzled. 'Then why ever
did you get me to come out?'

'So that we can sort out the
story in a more satisfactory way,'
explained the Little Dragon.

'Don't think I quite under-stand, old boy,' said Sir George. 'I think it's a dashed good story meself. Ends very well. Dragon dead, Princess saved, me a hero and about to get married to the girl. Nothing wrong with that!'

'Oh, yes there is,' came a female voice. They all looked at the book and there, climbing out of the pictures, was a beautiful Princess with long golden plaits. They all stared at the Princess.

The Little Dragon was the first to find his voice.

'Oh, well done, Sir George, you've got the Princess out as well. Now we really can get on with the business of rewriting this story.'

'I think that's a very good idea,' said the Princess. 'And *I* want to decide what happens to me.'

'You mean you don't want to marry me?' asked Sir George in a perplexed tone.

'Exactly,' said the Princess. 'Nothing personal, I just want to see the world a bit. If I do get married I want to choose the man, not marry him just because he's killed some rotten old Dragon.'

'You don't have to be rude,' said the Little Dragon. 'I'm not a rotten old Dragon and, after all, it's me that started this business of getting the story changed.'

'Sorry,' the Princess said apologetically. 'I got a bit carried away.'

Janet looked at the three little figures arguing on her tummy. She coughed softly to catch their attention.

'It seems to me,' she said, 'that if the Princess has decided not to marry Sir George, then he doesn't need to kill the Dragon in the first place.'

'Won't do,' Sir George interrupted. 'Not only the girl, you know. I mean, this Dragon has been terrorizing the whole country for years.'

'I'll stop it,' said the Little Dragon. 'I'll stop terrorizing the people and then you won't have to kill me.'

'That's all well and good,' said Sir George, 'but what about me, and what about my reputation? If I don't kill the Dragon then no one will hear about me.'

'I've got it!' said the Little Dragon with a shriek of triumph. 'Let's have a different villain in the story.'

'Sorry, old chap,' said Sir George. 'Slow up a bit, I'm not with you.'

'Yes,' agreed the Princess. 'Explain what you mean.'

'There's a terrible sea-monster,' explained the Dragon. 'He's causing all the trouble, all the rough seas, all the shipwrecks and everything. He's a really frightful creature. He's got sixteen feet and ten eyes and teeth like razors and he eats at least ten children a day. Are you with me?'

'So far, yes,' Sir George said.

' 'Course,' the Princess said.

'Now, because I'm such a clever Dragon I know where the sea-monster hides, right?'

They all nodded.

'So,' continued the Little Dragon, 'I go and tell the Princess where the sea-monster is. She is so angry that she wants to go and kill the monster (who is making her people miserable) with her own bare hands.'

'That's a good idea,' said the Princess. 'I like that.'

'Good,' said the Little Dragon. 'I thought you might. So the Princess jumps on the Dragon's back and off they go. On the way

they meet brave Sir George, an honest Knight whom everyone likes and admires.'

'Jolly good line that,' said Sir George approvingly. 'But dash it – killing sea-monsters is man's work. I mean, Princesses just sit around and look beautiful.'

'That's silly,' snorted the Princess. 'If you take that attitude I shall go back into the story.' She got up and, tossing her golden plaits over her shoulder, she moved towards the book.

'STOP!' yelled the Little Dragon. 'Princess, if you go back into the story you *will* have to marry Sir George. So why not let him have his way? He'll be all

upset if you don't let him kill the sea-monster.'

'Men!' groaned the Princess.

'Quite,' agreed the Dragon. 'But to get back to the story, Sir George kills the sea-monster with a lot of help from the Dragon and then . . .'

'Then what?' asked the Princess.

'Then the Dragon doesn't have to get killed and everyone lives happily ever after.'

'That won't do,' objected the

Princess. 'Just how do they live happily ever after?'

'Well, I don't know,' said the Little Dragon. 'I've done my bit, now you write the rest.'

'I know,' said the Princess. 'The Dragon and Sir George and the Princess get on so well that they set off together and have lots of lovely adventures.'

'Yes!' yelled Sir George. 'That would be simply splendid and then perhaps we could get married.'

'NO!' the Princess said. 'If that's a condition, NO.'

'Well, it's not a condition,' Sir George said. 'I was just hoping – you can't stop a chap hoping.'

'You can hope,' said the Princess, 'but no promises.'

'Fair enough,' agreed the Knight.

'Friends,' said the Little Dragon, 'it seems that the matter is now settled to everyone's satisfaction and we can therefore now return to our book.'

Janet felt very relieved to hear these words and held the book open while the three climbed in. She was just about to close the book tightly shut when the Little Dragon stuck his head out and said, 'By the way, thanks for your help.'

'Promise me before you go back,' said Janet urgently, 'that you'll never come out of this book again.'

'Shan't promise – shan't,' said the Little Dragon. 'I reserve my

right to come out of this story whenever I feel like it. I shall do exactly what I like when I like and there is nothing whatsoever you can do about it.' He blew a little flame at her and disappeared.

Chapter 5

The next morning Janet insisted that she felt a lot better and went off to school clutching her book. After the register had been taken, Janet's class was told to go to the school library and change their

books. Janet was worried that the Dragon, Sir George and the Princess might change their minds and come out of the story again. Quickly she put her book in the Returned Books tray.

Samantha Brown stood next to her.

'Feeling better today, Janet?' asked Samantha, giggling.

'Much better, thanks,' said

Janet. 'Why don't you take out the book I was reading? It's really good.'

'Looks boring,' Samantha said.

'It's not boring,' said Janet. 'Honest.'

'All right,' Samantha said, and she sat down at a table, opened the book and began flicking through it. Suddenly she shrieked!

'What's the matter, Samantha?' asked the librarian.

'This book,' said Samantha,

licking her hand. 'It burned me, and stuck a pin in me, and pulled my hair.'

'Don't be ridiculous, Samantha,' snapped the librarian, while the whole class laughed. 'Bring the book back to me and choose another one and stop being silly.'

As they filed out of the library Janet glanced at the book on the librarian's desk. The three figures on the cover smiled at her and waved.

They were trying to help me,

thought Janet. The Dragon burned her, the Knight pricked her, and the Princess pulled her hair. Oh dear, poor Samantha.

Janet ran out into the playground. Samantha was leaning against a wall on her own, trying not to cry. Janet went up to her.

'You OK, Sam?' she asked.

'Yes,' said Samantha tearfully, 'but they did burn me and prick me and pull my hair. No one believes me, but they did.'

'I know,' said Janet. 'I believe you, honestly.'

'Thanks, Jan,' Samantha said. 'Sorry I was so rotten to you yesterday.'

'Not to worry,' Janet replied. 'Come on, let's play rounders – I missed out yesterday.'

'Janet,' said Samantha, 'let's be friends?'

'I'd like that,' agreed Janet. 'Thanks, Little Dragon.'

'What's a dragon got to do with it?' asked Samantha.

'Nothing,' said Janet hurriedly. 'Come on, before we miss the game.'

THE END